ONE, TWO BUCKLE MY SHOE

A BOOK OF COUNTING RHYMES

ROWAN BARNES-MURPHY

HODDER AND STOUGHTON
LONDON SYDNEY AUCKLAND TORONTO

Dedicated to my friends and agents
Bud and Evelyne Johnson

British Library Cataloguing in Publication Data
One, two, buckle my shoe: a book of counting rhymes.
1. Nursery rhymes, English
I. Barnes-Murphy, Rowan
398'.8   PZ8.3

ISBN 0-340-42719-1

First published in Great Britain 1988 by arrangement with Simon & Schuster, Inc., New York

Published by Hodder and Stoughton Children's Books,
a division of Hodder and Stoughton Ltd,
Mill Road, Dunton Green, Sevenoaks, Kent TN13 2YJ

Manufactured in the United States of America

ONE, TWO BUCKLE MY SHOE

A BOOK OF COUNTING RHYMES

As I was going to St. Ives,
I met a man with seven wives,

Each wife had seven sacks,

Each sack had seven cats,

Each cat had seven kits:

Kits, cats, sacks, and wives,
How many were there going to St . Ives?

One, two, three, four, five, six, seven,
All good children go to heaven.
One, two, three, four, five, six, seven, eight,
All bad children have to wait.

Two legs sat upon
three legs
With one leg in his lap;
In comes four legs
And runs away with one leg;
Up jumps two legs,
Throws it after four legs,
And makes him bring back one leg.

I'll sing you a song,
Nine verses long,
For a pin:
Three and three are six,
And three are nine;
You are a fool,
And the pin is mine.

Cobbler, cobbler, mend my shoe,
Have it done by half past two.
If half past two is far too late,
Have it done by half past eight.
One, two, three, four,
Back, two, three, four,
Bake it, bake it, hammer, hammer, hammer.

Gregory Griggs, Gregory Griggs,
Had twenty-seven different wigs.
He wore them up, he wore them down,
To please the people of the town;
He wore them east, he wore them west,
But he never could tell which he loved the best.

There were two birds sat on a stone,

One flew away, and then there was one,

The other flew after, and then there was none,

And so the poor stone was left all alone,

There were three sisters in a hall
    Then came a knight amongst them all;
Good morrow, aunt, to the one,
Good morrow, aunt, to the other,
Good morrow, gentlewoman, to the third,
If you were an aunt, as the other two be,
I would say good morrow, then, aunts all three.

One, two, three, four,
    Mary at the cottage door,
Five, six, seven, eight,
Eating cherries off a plate.

Eeny, meeney,
      miney, mo,
Catch a tiger by the toe.
If he hollers let him go.
Eeeny, meeney, miney, mo.

There were three jovial
        Welshman,
As I have heard men say,
And they would go a-hunting
Upon St. David's day.

All the day they hunted
And nothing could they find,
But a hedgehog in a bramble bush,
And that they left behind.

The first said it was a hedgehog,
The second he said, Nay;
The third said it was a pincushion,
With the pin stuck in wrong way.

This old man, he played one,
He played nick nack on my drum.

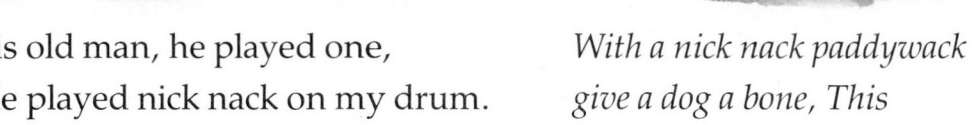

*With a nick nack paddywack
give a dog a bone, This
old man came rolling home.*

This old man, he played two,
He played nick nack on my shoe.

This old man, he played three,
He played nick nack on my knee.

This old man, he played four,
He played nick nack on my door.

This old man, he played five,
He played nick nack on a hive.

This old man, he played six,
He played nick nack with some sticks.

This old man, he played seven,
He played nick nack up in heaven.

This old man, he played eight,
He played nick nack on my gate.

This old man, he played nine.
He played nick nack on a line.

This old man, he played ten,
He played nick nack with a hen.

One old Oxford ox
opening oysters.

Two toads totally tired
trying to trot to Tisbury.

Three thick thumping tigers
taking toast for tea.

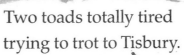

Four finicky fishermen
fishing for finny fish.

Five frippery Frenchmen
foolishly fishing for frogs.

Six sportsmen
shooting snipe.

Seven Severn salmon
swallowing shrimps.

Eight eminent Englishmen
eagerly examining Europe.

Nine nimble noblemen
nibbling nectarines.

Ten tinkering tinkers
tinkering ten tin tinder-boxes.

Eleven elephants
elegantly equipped.

Twelve typographical topographers
typically translating type.

My mother sent me for some water,
For some water from the sea,
My foot slipped, and in I tumbled,
Three jolly sailors came to me:
One said he'd buy me silks and satins,
One said he'd buy me a guinea gold ring,
One said he'd buy me a silver cradle
For to rock my baby in.

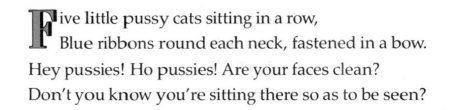

Five little pussy cats sitting in a row,
Blue ribbons round each neck, fastened in a bow.
Hey pussies! Ho pussies! Are your faces clean?
Don't you know you're sitting there so as to be seen?

Rub-a-dub-dub,
Three men in a tub,
And who do you think they be?
The butcher, the baker,
The candlestick-maker,
Turn 'em out, knaves all three.

Baa, baa, black sheep,
Have you any wool?
Yes, sir, yes, sir,
Three bags full;
One for the master,
And one for the dame,

And one for the little boy
Who lives down the lane.

One, two, three,
    four, five,
Once I caught a fish alive,
Six, seven, eight, nine, ten,
Then I let it go again.

Why did you let it go?
Because it bit my finger oh!
Which finger did it bite?
This little finger on the right.

I saw eight magpies in a tree,

Two for you and six for me:

One for sorrow, two for mirth,

Three for a wedding, four for a birth;

Five for England, six for France,

Seven for a fiddler, eight for a dance.

One, two,
Buckle my shoe;

Three, four,
Knock at the door;

Five, six,
Pick up sticks;

Seven eight,
Lay them straight;

Nine, ten,
A big fat hen;

Eleven, twelve,
Dig and delve;

Thirteen, fourteen,
Maids a-courting;

Fifteen, sixteen,
Maids in the kitchen;

Seventeen, eighteen,
Maids in waiting;

Nineteen, twenty,
My plate's empty.